Desperate For A Dog

Rose Impey and Jolyne Knox

Collins

Look out for more *Jets* from Collins

For Rachel and Holly

First published by A & C Black Ltd in 1988
Published by Collins in 1988
25 24 23 22 21 20 19 18 17
Collins is an imprint HarperCollins*Publishers* Ltd,
77–85 Fulham Palace Road, Hammersmith, London W6 8JB

The HarperCollins website address is
www.harpercollins.co.uk

ISBN 0 00 673007 8

Text © Rose Impey 1988
Illustrations © Jolyne Knox 1988

The author and the illustrator assert the moral right to be
identified as the author and the illustrator of the work.
A CIP record for this title is available from the British Library.
Printed and bound in Great Britain by Clays Ltd, St Ives plc

Round One

Me and my sister were desperate
for a dog.
All our friends had dogs.
Our cousin had a cat
and a rabbit
and a dog.

Half the people in our street had dogs.

Everyone except us.
We just had to have one.

First we asked our dad.
'Dad, can we have a dog?'
'Please?'

But he said,
'A dog? Oh no!
Certainly not.'
And he started
to laugh.
'But why?' we said.
'Why not?'
So Dad put down his saw
and he told us.
He gave us all sorts of reasons.

He counted them off on his fingers.
Against a dog . . .

1. Dogs make a mess

We'd clean it up.

2. Dogs are noisy.

We'd keep it quiet.

3. Dogs need lots of exercise.

We'd walk it.

4. Dogs cost money to feed.

We'd give up our pocket money.

5. You can't take dogs on holiday.

We'd stay at home.

6. Our house isn't big enough for a dog.

We could move!

'And number seven,' said Dad, 'who would look after it when you two are at school?

Me, of course.
I'd be the one at home with it.

And I don't even like dogs.

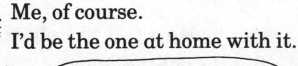

7

Well that was true.
He is the one at home all day.
Our dad's unemployed.
He doesn't go out to work.
He's always busy in his shed —
making things,
shelves and cupboards mostly.

Our house is full of cupboards.
But it's not the same.
He'd rather go to work.

'A dog would be company for you,'
I said, 'when you're on your own
all day.'

You could talk to it.

'A dog could be useful,' I said.
'You could teach it things.'
'Tricks,' she said.
'To fetch your tools,' I said.
'A dog can hold things in its mouth,'
my sister said.
And then she got carried away.

'I bet you could teach a clever dog to saw wood,

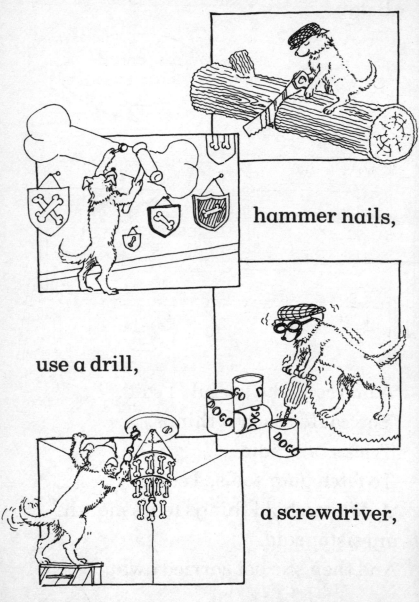

hammer nails,

use a drill,

a screwdriver,

a paintbrush,

hang wallpaper.

If it was really clever I bet it could
make its own kennel!'
Sometimes my sister is pretty
stupid.

Dad started to laugh.
'I suppose we'd call it D.I.Y. Dog,'
he said.
Then he laughed even harder.
Our dad always laughs most at
his own jokes.

'Come on,' I said. 'We'll go and ask
Mum.'

Mum was in the
spare bedroom —
wallpapering.

Please?

'Mu..u..m,' we said,
'can't we have
a dog?'

'You don't want a dog,' she said.
'You've got a pet already.'
Well that was true. We had.

But you can't take a hamster for a
walk on a lead, can you?

'It's not the same,' we said.
'We want a dog.'
'More than anything in the whole
wide world,' said my sister.

And her bottom lip went all wobbly.

Mum put the paste brush in the bucket.
She sat down for a break.

'Tell me why,' she said.
So we told her.
We tried to think of lots of reasons.
We started to count them off on our
fingers.

For a dog . . .

1. Dogs guard your house when you're out.

2. You can take a dog for walks.

3. Dogs are nice. You can have fun with them.

4 Erm...

Erm...

We couldn't seem to think of
any more.
So in the end we said,

WE JUST WANT ONE !

Please Mum ?

Please!

'Well,' said Mum,
'you'll have to ask
Dad. He's the one
at home all day.
It isn't really up to me.'

Then Dad came in.
We smiled at him.
'Da..a..d . . .'

Don't ask!
I've told you once.
The answer's no.
..N..O... no.
Certainly not.
Out of the question.
Absolutely.. no.. no..
..no...no...no..
..,no.....
NO!

You could tell he meant it.
My sister burst out crying.

Oh dear Dad's very dogmatic!

End of Round One.

Round Two

A few weeks later, just before my
sister's birthday, we went to stay
with Grandma and Grandad.
We went in the car.
The journey passed really quickly.

Me and my sister made up
a new game.
We called it 'Spot The Dog'.

As Mum drove along we looked out
of the car windows.
We made a list of how many dogs
we saw and what kind they were,
and what colour.
Then we pretended they were our
dogs and we chose names for them.

1 Queeny a brown labrador
2 Benjie a black spaniel
3 Coco a brown sausage dog
4 Capt Hook a white sheepdog
5 Steak and kidney a
   brown and white mongerel

6

The rule was that we could only
count dogs on our own side of
the road.
It's hard writing in a car, especially
when you go round corners.

'Dad,' I said, 'how do you spell
Weetabix?'
'You're going to call a dog
Weetabix?' asked Dad.

'That Airedale
over there.
It's just
like Weetabix,
light brown and
crunchy.' I said.

'It's not crunchy when the milk's on it,' said my sister.
'It's all sloppy like a bowl of . . .'

'That's enough,' said Mum. 'We've heard that before.'
'It is though, isn't it?' said Dad, thinking about it.
'Oh, don't start her off,' said Mum.
'Just spell Weetabix will you.'

My sister can hardly spell anything.
She did little drawings instead.

By the time we turned into Grandma's
estate I'd counted eight dogs.
My sister had six.

We started to argue about one that crossed from her side to mine. Mum had to slow down to miss it.

'Can't you two talk about anything else?' said Mum. 'You've got dogs on the brain.'

'But that's *my* dog,' I said.

'If it keeps on walking out in front of cars,' said Dad, 'it'll soon be a dead dog.'

'That's not funny,' I said.

'Horrid,' said my sister.

In the end we both counted it.

When we looked up we were
already there.
Grandma and Grandad were
standing at the gate waving.

After tea, when we were ready for bed, Grandad said to my sister, 'Well, little cough-drop, have you decided what you want for your birthday?'

Grandad always calls us funny names.

Mum and Dad say he spoils us.

I think he spoils my sister most.

My sister said,
'It's a secret. I want to whisper.'
And she climbed onto his knee.
She whispered in his ear.
Grandad began to smile.
'Is that all?' he said.
She just nodded.

'What's going on?' said Dad.
But my sister said,
'It's private.'

On her birthday my sister had lots of parcels.

Grandad's was the smallest.
She left it till the very last.
When she opened it her face went bright pink.

It was a collar and lead.
'But we haven't even got a dog,'
I said.
'Not yet, we haven't,' she said,
in a really cheeky way.
And because it was her birthday
Dad didn't say anything.

My sister started grinning.

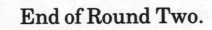

End of Round Two.

Round Three

Every Saturday we have
a local paper.
It comes about five o'clock.
Dad likes to look at it first, to read
the football results.

Mum likes to see what's on at the
pictures and if there's anyone she
knows in the local news.
She takes ages.
She works in a library.

She has to read lots of books,
but she must be a slow reader.

'Can't you hurry up, Mum?' we said.
'We want to read the paper.'

'You do?' said Mum. 'Whatever for?'
'The adverts,' we said.
'You are a funny pair,' she said.
But she handed it over.

Then my sister and I
sat together on the sofa.
We each held up one
side of the paper.
We turned towards
the back.
At the top of the page
was an enormous word.
I couldn't read it.

'Miscellaneous Sales,'
said Mum.
There were long lists
of things people were
trying to sell:
cement mixers and
prams and greenhouses
and second-hand fur
coats and videos.
But the last row said,
'Pet's Corner'.

Here it is.

I began to read them out to my sister. We put rings round the best ones with black felt pen.

Pets Corner

Free to a good home, Labrador dog 4 years. Tel. 682708

Persian kittens, ready now. Tel. 915677

Parrot Boarding. Good care and attention. Treated as own pets. All types of birds at fair prices. Tel. 238971

Collie Puppies, ready now or wait till Christmas. Tel. 603224

Pick of the litter — Great Dane puppies, blues, blacks and harlequins. Real dog lovers only. Tel. 72777

THE·DOG·HOUSE Boarding Kennels — Many satisfied clients. Call— Tel. 565642

Jack Russell pups — very small £25 also nice pony. Tel. 701698

Good homes for Tabby kittens Twelve weeks. Tel. 495061

Kitty Litter — 10 lb bags delivered to your door. Call now. Tel. 896053

Double buggy, stair gate, 4 chairs, tropical fish and sandwich-maker. Tel. 365421

As new - Dropside Cot, Cosytoes, Kiddie Carrier, Camping Cot and Baby Nest. Tel. 51826

General

For sale. 3 man tent, sandpit with cover and a very large house pla[...] Tel. 235678

Tortoise Help Line- Any problems and advice. Ring 372444

SHE[...] ca[...] T[...]

36

'For goodness sake,' said Dad, 'You sound like a pair of pigeons. Now stop reading those stupid adverts and come and have tea.'

At bedtime my sister and I took the paper upstairs with us. Instead of a bedtime story I read her the adverts.

Last of the litter
Sheltie puppy (bitch)
- must find home
soon.
Looking for someone
to love her.
Tel. 696487
    6—10 pm.

When I'd finished she said, 'Read me the one about the sheltie puppy again.'

Then she said to me,
'Let's ring it.'
'What do you mean?' I said.
'Let's ring the number – 696487 –
on the phone.'
So we did.

We crept along the landing and
used the phone in Mum's new study.
We talked very quietly so Mum and
Dad wouldn't hear. The lady on the
phone told us all about the puppy. It
sounded so cute.
'Ahhhhhhh,' I said.
'Ohhhhhhh,' said my sister.
We talked to her for ages.
Then we crept back to bed.

The next day we were just sitting
down for lunch when
the doorbell rang.
Mum went to the door.
Then she called Dad.
It was the lady from the paper.
She'd brought the puppy with her.

Mum looked red. She didn't know
what to say.
Dad looked red. He had plenty to say.

It was very naughty of you to waste that lady's time. I've told you before we are not having a dog. Certainly not. No chance. When I say no — I mean no. And I will not change my mind. Now do you understand?

One up to Dad!

My sister burst out crying again.

End of Round Three.

Round Four

Not long after
that a wonderful
thing happened.
Well, it was
wonderful for me
and my sister.
It wasn't very nice
for Mrs. Roper,
the lady who lives
next door.

She had to go into
hospital to have an
operation. Me and
my sister made
get well cards and
sent them with
Mum when
she visited.

The **wonderful** part of it

was that we had to look after
her dog!
Toby was a big black labrador.
He was quite old, in dog years.
He'd never been in kennels.

Mrs. Roper refused to go into
hospital until Mum promised that
we'd look after Toby.

Dad wasn't very pleased.
'Dogs,' he said. 'I'm sick of hearing about dogs. Still, I suppose it will make some people happy.'

We couldn't stop laughing
when Mum told us.

It's okay for you but I'm the one at home all day. I'll have to look after the old fleabag.

'Oh, Dad!' we said.
Even Mum was shocked.

'It was a joke,' said Dad.

Oh Dad!

45

Me and my sister would have been
happy to stay at home all day
with Toby.
In fact each morning my sister said

she had a tummy ache

or a cold coming

or a sore ankle.

Dad wasn't fooled once.
Every day he made her go to school.

But each night when we got home

We washed Toby's bowls

and mixed his food

DOG

and brushed his coat

and took him for walks.

When he was in a good mood
Toby would chase a stick or a ball,
if it didn't go too far.
He never brought it back.
Toby didn't really like exercise.

Mostly Toby liked to sleep.
Sometimes he slept in his basket in
the kitchen.

Sometimes he slept in front
of the gas fire.

And sometimes he slept right
against the fence as close as he
could get to his own home.

When we were at school, Toby liked
to sleep in Dad's shed.
'He's always there under my feet,'
Dad complained.

At teatime each day Dad told us
stories about what Toby had done
that day:

how he'd chewed
the handle off
Dad's best
screwdriver,

or dug holes in
the flower-bed
to bury bits of
Dad's wood,

or eaten a whole tin of wax polish
and then been sick in the sandpit.

We thought they were funny
stories. But Dad didn't.
'That dog would eat anything,'
said Dad. 'He must be the thickest dog
in the world. I don't think
he's got anything
between his ears
except sawdust.'

After Toby had been with
us for three weeks he felt
like one of the family.
Mum saved all the scraps
for him. She made a real
fuss of him.
Even Dad stopped moaning.
He didn't exactly seem
to like Toby,
he just put up with him.

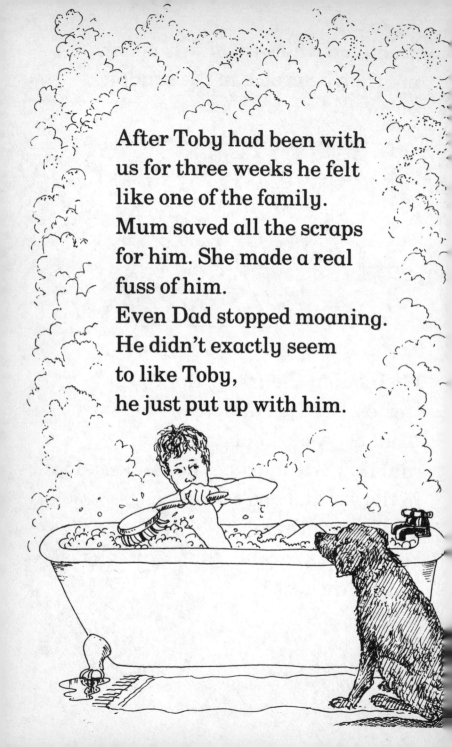

But Toby certainly liked
Dad. He followed him
everywhere. When Dad
sat down in the evening
Toby shuffled up and lay
down on Dad's feet like a
black velvet foot-warmer.

One day me and
my sister ran all
the way home from
school. To see how
fast we could do it.

We raced into the house to surprise Dad.
We could hardly believe our eyes.
Dad and Toby were rolling on the
floor playing a silly game.
Dad was laughing his
head off and pushing
Toby in a
really friendly way.
Toby was trying
to bite
Dad's ear.

When Dad saw us he went red.
He looked so embarrassed . . .
seeing us . . . seeing him . . .
fooling about with Toby.

I thought you said Toby was an old fleabag with no brains.

I thought you said you didn't like dogs.

You're a fibber!

Dad said nothing.

What could he say?
We'd caught him out.
He couldn't fool us anymore.
Me and my sister stood there grinning.

Woof Woofee!
I'll be Top Dog yet.

End of Round Four.

The Final Round

Soon after that Mrs. Roper came out of hospital. The day she came home we tied a big bow and a 'Welcome Home' sign around Toby's neck. We made Mrs. Roper a cup of tea and stayed for a while to keep her company.

When we got home
our own house
seemed so quiet
and empty, as if
something was missing.

Something *was* missing
and it was Toby.
Dad tried to be
cheerful.

'Isn't it nice and quiet?' he said.
'You can see the fire for a change.

No more dog hairs.
No more biscuits
down the chairs.
Back to normal
at last.'

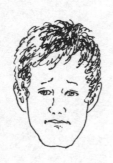

But nobody felt cheered up.
'Don't go on,' said Mum.

In bed that night my sister
began to cry.
She was missing Toby.
Mum leaned on the bed and held
her hand.
'You can still take him for walks,'
she said.
But the next day, when we called
round.

Toby refused to move.
He didn't even look at us.
Now he'd got Mrs. Roper back
he wasn't going to leave her
for a minute.

The rest of the week was really dull.
When we came in from school there
was no one to look after or take
for a walk.

At teatime Dad had no funny
stories to tell us. In fact nobody
seemed to have anything to say at all.

On Friday we sat at the tea table.
I didn't feel very hungry.
My sister was making funny faces
with her salad.

Mum wasn't eating much either.

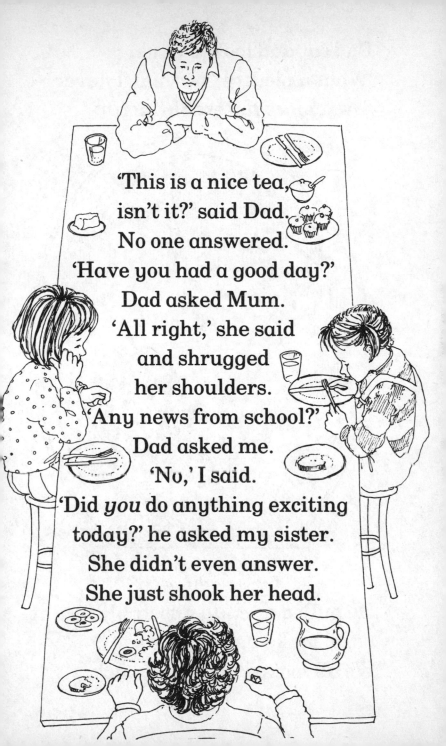

'This is a nice tea, isn't it?' said Dad. No one answered. 'Have you had a good day?' Dad asked Mum. 'All right,' she said and shrugged her shoulders. 'Any news from school?' Dad asked me. 'No,' I said. 'Did *you* do anything exciting today?' he asked my sister. She didn't even answer. She just shook her head.

Dad sat and looked at us.
'What a picture,' he said. 'I never saw a more miserable family.'

The Most Miserable
Family in the World

He pulled a really miserable face at us, to make us laugh.
We all looked miserable back.

Cheer up! We nearly threw a party.

Yippee!

And the very next day
we went to choose a dog.